Ruth Miskin's
Superphonics®
Green Storybook

Bull in a
China Shop

by Gill Munton

Illustrated by Guy Parker-Rees

Hodder
Children's
Books

a division of Hachette Children's Books

Mr. Chadwick was in his shop,
unpacking some big boxes.
They were full of jugs and glasses.

"I need some help in this shop!"
he said.

Superphonics *Storybooks* will help your child to learn to read using Ruth Miskin's highly effective phonic method. Each story is fun to read and has been carefully written to include particular sounds and spellings.

The Storybooks are graded so your child can progress with confidence from easy words to harder ones. There are four levels - Blue (the easiest), Green, Purple and Turquoise (the hardest). Each level is linked to one of the core *Superphonics* Books.

ISBN: 978 0 340 79894 2

Text copyright © 2002 Gill Munton
Illustrations copyright © 2002 Guy Parker-Rees

Editorial by Gill Munton
Design by Sarah Borny

The rights of Gill Munton and Guy Parker-Rees to be identified as the author and illustrator of this Work have been asserted by them in accordance with the Copyright, Designs and Patents Act 1988.

First published in Great Britain 2002

10 9 8 7 6 5 4

First published in 2002 by Hodder Children's Books,
a division of Hachette Children's Books,
338 Euston Road, London NW1 3BH
An Hachette UK Company. www.hachette.co.uk

Printed and bound in China by WKT Company Ltd.

A CIP record is registered by and held at the British Library.

Target words

All the Green Storybooks focus on the following sounds:

Double consonants,
e.g. **ll** as in **bull**

Blended consonants,
e.g. **ng** as in **rang**

Two or three consonants together,
e.g. **sm** as in **smash**, **lp** as in **help**

These target words are featured in the book:

add	glasses	Chadwick
assistant	off	chicks
bell	sell	clocks
bills	till	cluck
bottom	umbrella	dusting
bull	wallop	having
bulls	well	hung
called	will	inspecting
cross(ly)	yelled	ping
eggs		rang
full	back	sacked
fuss	bang	scratching

unpack	felt	pink
unpacking	grunt	rest
	help	shelf
and	himself	smash
basket	just	stand
best	lamps	step
cloth	last	thank
crash	must	think
dust	next	went

(Words containing sounds and spellings practised in the Blue Storybooks have been used in the story, too.)

Other words

Also included are some common words (e.g. **what**, **where**) which your child will be learning in his or her first few years at school.

A few other words have been used to help the story to flow.

Reading the book

1 Make sure you and your child are sitting in a quiet, comfortable place.

2 Tell him or her a little about the story, without giving too much away:

Mr Chadwick is trying to find someone to help him in his china shop ...

This will give your child a mental picture; having a context for a story makes it easier to read the words.

3 Read the target words (above) together. This will mean that you can both enjoy the story without having to spend too much time working out the words. Help your child to sound out each word (e.g. **b-u-ll**) before saying the whole word.

4 Let your child read the story aloud. Help him or her with any difficult words and discuss the story as you go along. Stop now and again to ask your child to predict what will happen next. This will help you to see whether he or she has understood what has happened so far.

Above all, enjoy the story, and praise your child's reading!

He wrote on a card:

WANTED:
shop assistant
Must be good at maths
and dusting

He stuck the card on the door.

The next day, the shop bell rang -
ping! - and in came a hen.

"I've come about the job," she said.
"How much will you pay me?"

"Never mind about that,"
said Mr. Chadwick.
"Can you add up bills?
Can you wash and dust?"

"Oh, I can do all that,"
said the hen,
inspecting a set of egg cups.

"Well, then," said Mr. Chadwick,
"you can start right away.
Dust all the dishes and the cups.
Don't smash them!

Crash!
Bang!
Wallop!

Then sell as much as you can.
Put all the cash in the till."

But when Mr. Chadwick came back,
the hen was not there.
There was no cash in the till.
All the dishes and cups were dusty.

"Hen!" he called crossly.

"Where are you?

What did you sell today?"

"Cluck!"

There was the hen,
sitting on six eggs
in Mr. Chadwick's
best umbrella stand.

"What's all the fuss?" she said.
"Just look at these eggs!
I'm going to have six chicks!"

"You're sacked!" said Mr. Chadwick

The next day,

the shop bell rang again -

ping! - and in came a pig.

"I've come about the job," he said.

"How many days off will I get?"

"Never mind about that,"
said Mr. Chadwick.
"Can you unpack boxes?
Can you dust shelves?"

"Oh, I can do all that,"
said the pig, scratching
his fat pink bottom on a shelf.

"Well, then," said Mr. Chadwick,
"you can start right away.
Dust all the dishes and cups.
Don't smash them!

Crash!
Bang!
Wallop!

Then sell as much as you can.
Put all the cash in the till."

But when Mr. Chadwick came back,

the pig was not there.

There was no cash in the till.

All the dishes and cups were dusty.

"Pig!" he called crossly.

"Where are you?

What did you sell today?"

"Grunt!"

There was the pig,
having a rest in Mr. Chadwick's
best picnic basket.

"What's all the fuss?" he said.
"I've had a lovely nap!"

"You're sacked!" said Mr. Chadwick.

"I wish I could find a shop assistant," said Mr. Chadwick to himself. "Those two were no good at all."

And then the shop bell rang - ping! - and in came a bull!

"No bulls!" yelled Mr. Chadwick.

"Can't you read?

Bulls and china shops

just don't mix!"

The bull looked sad.

"I've been to all the shops

I can think of," he said.

"This is the last one.

No one wants a bull

for a shop assistant -

I can't think why.

Please will you give me a job,

Mr. Chadwick?"

Mr. Chadwick felt sorry for the bull.

"Very well," he said.

"Let's see how you get on.

Dust all the dishes and the cups.

Don't smash them!

Then sell as much as you can.

Put all the cash in the till."

The bull went to the back
of the shop and got a cloth.

He dusted all the dishes
and he dusted all the cups.
He didn't smash one.

Then he waited for the bell
to go ping.

The bull sold lots of dishes ...

... and lots of cups ...

... and mugs ...

... and glasses ...

... and jugs ...

... and lamps ...

... and clocks.

He put lots of cash in the till.

When Mr. Chadwick came back,
he said, "Thank you, bull!
You've made me very rich!"

He went up to the bull,
to pat him on the back.

"Don't step on that cloth!"
yelled the bull.

But ...

Crash!
Bang!
Wallop!